The P Institute

Institute

Magnus Gray

This book is dedicated to my cousin Annabel. She is absolutely amazing and brave and fantastic. In fact I would even say she is PERFECT.

PROLOGUE

Orchard House at the end of Swithens Street was small and cosy. The white bricks on the outline of the wall were filled with colour and joy. The chimney puffed out smoke like an on-going train never filling up for coal. The flowers in the bright front garden brought serenity and delight into the setting. The windows shone brightly in the sun as it beat down on the estate. The sound of beautiful music drifted through the lane and in earshot of other houses. The sound was coming from *Orchard House*. The little house that loves to show beauty.

Samuel was sitting upright, rocking slowly side to side to the temperate beat of Beethoven's *Fur Elise*. He closed his eyes taking in the sound of the perfect piece. When he thought the time was so, he turned the page of the music book, which fluttered alive like a swift butterfly. The notes glided out of the piano and finding a place to pop like a bubble once they finished playing. Philip, only being 12, was reading Homer's *Iliad*. His eyes focused on the small font on the rough, old paper. He nodded his head as he understood that the focus of the book was about The Warrior Achilles. His eyes darted about when a new line began, which was quite often, as that the lines are quite short.

In the living room, Pamela, the mother of these two children, was resting her eyes, snug on the reclining chair. She slid her hand swiftly under the side of the chair, reaching for the button. She found it, gently pressed it and held on to it. The bottom of the chair slowly lifted its way up until it could no more. She smiled and took in a deep breath. Then she released.

She smiled once more and went to sleep listening to the relaxing piano music of her perfect son, and thinking about how clever her other son is. And tomorrow, she knew would be a good day: her perfectly taught daughter will be coming home from The Perfect Institute. Their perfect family would be complete.

Chapter 1

The sound of crying babies surrounded the room. Severe looking nurses leaned over the babies. The baby softened its crying, and in a moment of terror showed lovely, soft red gums. After giving the baby a sharp injection, the nurse pulled a silly face and the baby laughed or cried in terror – it was hard to tell.

Inside the building it was incredibly bright. The bright light shone hugely down on the babies. The walls were brown and covered with tints of pink to lighten the babies up. Overall, there were about 100 babies in the small room. Cots were everywhere, filled with small bodies of joy (or fear it – was hard to tell). The nurse refilled the injection and moved on to the next cot.

Sophie's knees were shaking. Her head was light and filled with trauma and fear. She kept turning round in circles and wondering what on Earth she had just experienced. A big, lumbering man in a white suit came towards the line of children. A boy who was behind her lightly pushed her out of the way and pushed in front of her. Sophie frowned but didn't say anything. The man was now in the front of the long line of children. He was carrying some more pills. He then started giving the first few people the oblong shaped pellet. Sophie looked at the first boy who was given the red and yellow pill. His reaction was strange. His eyebrows moved upwards in surprise and then he started blinking. Then his face went blank. He then looked around, wondering where he was. Sophie immediately knew what this pill was. It was a memory pill. Sophie frowned. She was clever. She read in a book once (before it was taken away from her) that the name Sophie meant 'Wisdom'. She knew what they were doing to them. She knew what the right thing was to do. And that was to do the *exact* opposite of what they wanted of her.

The man in the white suite finally reached her, the 89th child in the line of hundreds of children. The man slid out the pill and gave it to Sophie. He made a gesture making it obvious that Sophie had to eat it. Sophie then placed it gently onto her tongue and slid it back into place inside her mouth. She then pretended to swallow the pill, but in the doing so she put the pill under her tongue. The man did another gesture intending for Sophie to open her mouth, to show if she had swallowed it. Sophie's heart beat wildly inside her chest. She hesitantly opened her mouth wide. The man peered inside and then nodded and moved onto the next child. Sophie then breathed out a sigh of massive relief. After all the pills were taken, the line started to walk forward.

Chapter 2

In synchronization, the long line of boys and girls started to trudge slowly forward out of the bright building. The boy who had pushed in front of her, was now confused and dazed. So was everyone else. Except Sophie Newton. The pill was still embedded in the bottom of her mouth, sitting still without any problem. The man at the front leading the line of confused 10-year-olds reached out in front of him and grabbed the big door handle of the towering double doors. Sophie was shuddering and nervous. She hadn't been outside for almost 10 years.

The man twisted the door handle and hauled it open. The light shone brightly. Even brighter than it was inside. She shielded her eyes with her forearm as she put one foot in front of the other. The others were doing the same thing as Sophie as it was impossible not to. She took her first breath of the new, fresh air as they all stepped outside. Sophie then looked down the line and up the line to see if anyone was watching. She then put her fingers in her mouth and took out the pill. She then dropped it and crushed it with the heel of her foot. The man then stopped the line. He slid out another packet of pills. He started to give them out to everyone. When it got to her, she did the same process as before. Given the pill, slot it into her mouth, hide it under her tongue, then spit and then crunch under her heel.

Sophie looked back when she exited the building. There was a sign which read clearly: THE PERFECT INSTITUTE. Sophie shivered as she recalled over the years what had happened. Obviously, no one else remembered because of the pills they had just taken. But she did. Sophie remembered every miserable detail.

Parents dropped their children off at The Perfect Institute as soon as they were born and then they were taught to be PERFECT. Absolutely perfect. They were taught to do things nonstop. They were taught to be polite. To play the piano and another instrument. To learn Latin, Ancient Greek and another language. They were taught all sports. They were taught to cook, clean and tidy up. They were taught never to argue or answer back. They were taught how to write neatly and never spill food. They were taught how to hoover and scrub the floors and the toilets. They were taught how to weed in the garden and mend stuff. In short, they were taught how to be PERFECT children.

If they did anything wrong, horrific things happened to them. Such as: if they lied, the people in white suits, would force you onto a chair. You would try and struggle but there would be no point. They pinned you down onto a chair and then they viciously bound your mouth open and demand you to stick out your tongue. As you do so, they wrapped a wire around your tongue. You struggle until you can no more. They then calmly press a button and that sends a horrible shockwave through the nerves in your tongue. You scream out in horror as they send many more.

Sophie shuddered even thinking of what had happened to her. They beat you until you are perfect.

Chapter 3

There was a huge crowd of adults waiting for their perfect child to exit the Perfect Institute. Everyone in the line was excited and keen. The pill had been an excitement pill. The children didn't know anything about what happened but only knew they were excited to see their parents.

But Sophie knew. Sophie knew that she, and all of the children, had been tormented for 10 whole years. She knew that they had been given no love. She knew that the children had been tortured until they became perfect. Surely her parents would be horrified at what had happened to her. They would surely never give up a pure innocent baby to such an revolting institute if they knew the truth of what happened inside. Sophie knew that she had to tell her parents everything.

Sophie watched all the children meet up with their parents until there was only one woman standing impatiently alone. Sophie smiled and ran up to her mother and collapsed into her arms. Tears immediately poured down her face as she buried her head in a mother's shoulder. The tears started to dampen Pamela's cardigan. Pamela frowned and then shrugged off Sophie. Pamela thought, this is *not* the perfect daughter I was expecting. Crying. What's wrong with her? Pamela held Sophie by her shoulders and then told her that it was time to go home.

Sophie felt a wave of horror running through her. Her mother was disappointed in her. Her mother would not care what had happened to her.

Sophie had no choice. She pretended to be perfect and walked silently beside her mother to her car.

"It is good to finally meet you mother," Sophie said robotically.

"That's better," said Pamela. "It is good to meet my perfect daughter. I have two perfect sons – your perfect brothers. And now I have you. We shall be the *perfect* family."

Sophie pretended to smile. She took one last look at the forbidding Perfect Institute and faced her new, *perfect* future.

They arrived at Orchard House at the end of Swithens Street. The front garden was beautiful. Flowers were sprouting everywhere, obviously very well taken care of (Sophie realised her brothers probably did all of the gardening). The pretty flowers brought a bit of joy to Sophie. The sun shone brightly as she was still adjusting to the outside world. She heard the delightful sound of Fur Elise, by the famous composer Beethoven. She opened the red door and stepped inside her new life.

Inside the house, was a utility room. Sophie used the boot jack to swiftly slide off her shoes. She then neatly put them on the rack next to the other pairs of shoes. She then took a couple more steps. She twitched her nose smelling something good. She turned right intending to follow the smell. This led her into the kitchen where a boy was stood next to the hob, cooking something in the pan. It smelled like curry to her. The boy turned around and smiled as he saw his little sister for the first time. He walked up to her and gave her a hug. Sophie didn't really know what to do, because hugging this boy who was her brother, felt like a stranger because she had never met him before. His grip was soft against her body. It was a perfect hug. Just like she had been taught. He let go of Sophie and smiled a perfect smile.

"I'm Philip. It's a pleasure to meet my little sister after all these years." He then turned away and carried on stirring the mixture. Sophie sauntered through the kitchen, glancing at all the neatly arranged kitchen resources. It was all in the perfectly organised way she was taught. Big pans at the bottom of the line and small pans at the top. The kitchen table was laid out already for the curry. Fork on the left of the plate mat and knife on the right, then glasses on the top right of the knife. You could hear the fan and work of the dishwasher as it tumbled through the dirty crockery. Sophie placed her hand on the door handle where she twisted it and pushed it open. The soft piano music immediately wriggled into her ear. She recognized the piece; it was a lovely piece by a fantastic musician known as Clementi. The piece repeats itself but plays it in reverse. The boy had his eyes closed rocking to the beat. Pamela tapped him lightly on the shoulder. He smiled and then glanced at Sophie. His smile lit up even more. Sophie couldn't resist smiling herself.

The boy got up from his stool and hugged Sophie, just like Philip did. This boy was a lot taller that Philip and herself, so her face just went into his chest. He let go after about 10 seconds and smiled again.

"I'm Samuel. It's a pleasure to meet my little sister after all these years." He then turned back to the piano and carried on playing. She plodded on into another room, to see her father, David, sitting on a reclining chair, with his glasses at the tip of his nose, eyeing up a newspaper. He looked to see who had entered the room. He looked closer as he saw Sophie and grinned. He pushed his glasses back up to the bridge of his nose and slowly stood up. He walked to Sophie, still smiling, and embraced her into a hug. He released her and said:

"I'm so glad to meet you after all the years which have drifted by." He hugged her again. He then let go and sat back down.

"Come and sit down and talk to me about what you want to do tomorrow."

As Sophie approached her father, Philip entered the room to announce that dinner was served.

Sophie took a sip of her water. Her tongue was still sore after the incident. Everyone was eating while looking at her, waiting for her to say something.

David was the first to speak.

"So how were the years, Sophie?"

Then Pamela lightly hit David on the shoulder.

"She doesn't know what happened! Remember!" She muttered.

David nodded. Sophie had heard what she has said. Sophie then spoke. Her voice was soft and delicate, like a butterfly wing.

"I do remember, actually." She looked down on the floor, dreading to see their reactions. "I remember it all."

Chapter 4

Pamela looked confused, she looked over at David, who just shrugged.

"What do you mean, honey?"

Tears started to well up in Sophie's eyes. She lunged at her mother and wrapped her arms tightly around Pamela. Sophie was blubbering.

"It was horrible in there! They whipped us! They electrocuted us! They beat us until we were perfect!" Sophie then let out an almighty sob.

Pamela frowned, not properly understanding. She pushed Sophie off and held her by the shoulders. Sophie looked up at her mother's face. She was angry and she could tell that from miles away.

"What do you mean! It was amazing!" said Philip.

"We did all kinds of awesome stuff," said Samuel.

"I hated it! Absolutely hated it!" Tears poured down her face. Pamela got up and rushed over to the telephone and started to dial a number. It rang for a bit and then a manly voice came on to the phone.

"Hello? This is The Perfect Institute; how can I help?"

"Whatever you have done it has not worked! My child has just come back, talking about ridiculous things, which isn't *perfect* at all!" Pamela was almost screaming at this point. "I have to send her back."

"No!" Sophie screamed. She then jumped off her chair and ran out of the house.

Sophie's feet were patting down on the hard pavement. She was panting and she had a painful stitch in the side of her stomach. She stopped and wiped her forehead and then bent down and put her hand on her knees. She panted and then hauled herself up. She then remembered, that at The Perfect

Institute, she had a friend called Ellie. She had to find her. She ran on until she could no more. She looked around at her surroundings. The houses were all matching. They were all white and in the same formation. There was a girl painting a flower in her front garden. It was excellent. Then she looked closer and realized that it was Ellie! She ran up and said "Hi!". Ellie jumped and wiped her paintbrush all over the painting, leaving a depressing smudge of paint smeared across the painting. Ellie frowned and then smiled.

"Hi, Sophie! How are you?" She said this with a creepy smile spreading across her face.

"Sorry about your painting," Sophie said.

"Oh, it's okay, it is just a painting. Wasn't it so fun at The Perfect Institute?"

"What do you mean?"

"We learnt lots of different things at the institute! It was amazing. They were so kind to us as well."

Sophie couldn't believe her ears. The memory pill didn't wipe out all memories, it only wiped-out bad ones. She shook her head in desperation. What's happening? She turned and ran off listening to Ellie saying things about it being lovely to see her again. Sophie covered her ears as she ran.

Sophie carried on running, turning and twisting her head on the way trying to see where she was. She stopped and wiped a small piece of snot clinging from her nose. She slid her hand along her cheek trying to dry away the tears, but they just kept on coming. She checked her surroundings trying to figure out whereabouts she was. She walked on looking at the identical houses. Four windows at the front, all in different corners of the wall. The house she was looking at was painted white, just like the rest of them in the neighbourhood. She then peeked through one of the windows. A girl about her age was sitting up straight gracefully playing piano. The posture, the lovely plaits; they were perfect. Then she focused out of the room and looked properly at the window. She saw another girl about her age, with plaits and whitened teeth, with a flowery dress on. She then realised to her horror that she was staring at herself. She gasped in shock as she ruffled up her hair with her hands and ripped holes in the dress.

Sophie ran on and on. Eventually, she saw a sign for Swithens Street and knew she was on the right track. She ran to the end until she came upon the house that she would be living in for the rest of her life. She took a deep breath and ran straight into the house. She ran through the kitchen where Pamela was sitting, still on the phone. She hurled the phone on the ground and tried to grab Sophie, but Sophie dodged and crawled quickly up the stairs. She vaulted into her room and slammed the door shut.

Chapter 5

Sophie was sitting on her bed, slouched with baggy, purple eyes. She let out a sigh and then slouched even lower. She flicked her hair back behind her ear, with her hand and felt the lump in her throat begin to dim down. She heard a thump. Then another. Someone was coming up the stairs. She slid into her bed and covered up herself intending that no-one would see her. The door was knocked three times, and then there was a pause. Sophie peeked out from her duvet, seeing the door creak slowly open. She darted back under the covers. Someone entered the room. Is this someone from The Perfect Institute? No, it was David, her father. He patted her back gently. She didn't move. David patted her again. Sophie wormed around slowly and then poked her eyes out of the covers. She saw David's long face and dark, brown eyes. He smiled and stood up. Sophie emerged from the covers and leaned against the wall.

"What's the matter?" David asked nicely.

"I'm just scared," Sophie said.

"Of what?"

"Everything. Everyone is so perfect and I'm not. What's happened? I didn't want to eat the pill he gave us, I didn't want to get beaten, and I didn't want any of this to happen!" Sophie then realized what she had done. She had said everything to her own Dad! This will increase the chances of her going back to The Perfect Institute. She looked worryingly at David. He had no expression on his face. That was strange. Earlier, Pamela burst into tears and was shocked incredibly easily.

"Are you not worried for me? Are you going to send me back? Am I going to get beaten again?" Sophie burst into tears. David then leaned in and put his arms gently around Sophie's body. Sophie leant in as well and placed her head onto David's shoulder. Tears escaping rapidly from her cheeks and dropping to the floor. David stroked her back and soothed her gently.

"No one's going to do that to you. Ever. If they do, I'm going with you and protecting you all the way there." David felt Sophie nod slowly.

They then separated and looked at one another, dead on in the eyes. There was silence for a while. David was the first to speak.

"I have something to tell you."

"What is it?"

"I was exactly like you, if not worse."

Sophie frowned.

"You see, Sophie. I didn't eat the memory pill, I pretended to, just like you. Then I spat it out on the ground and crushed it with my foot. I remembered everything, the beating, the lies, and the perfectness. Everything. Moreover, I'm going to help you. We need to hatch a plan, and quick."

Chapter 6

"Why did you let me, Philip and Samuel go to the Institute even though you knew it was horrid?"

"That's a very good question. The honest answer is that most people hate children. Bringing them up well is the hardest job in the world so most parents just find it easier to send them to The Perfect Institute."

"But you seem nice Dad, why did you let us go?"

David sighed. "Pamela is very bossy, she loved her job in the office and didn't want to look after you herself. She said no decent person should be made to change nappies, teach children to eat nicely, or listen to hours of hideous music practice. She wanted to lead a life of fancy restaurants and nice clothes and said that having young children around would spoil all of that. I tried to think of excuses to not let you all go, but none of them worked. And if I'm honest, I also like nice restaurants."

"Oh, right." Sophie looked deflated.

"Couldn't you have looked after us Dad?"

"Me? I can barely look after myself."

"This sucks."

"I'm so sorry Sophie. I should have been a better parent."

Sophie looked at him. His face looked like a sad puppy's.

"You're forgiven."

David squeezed her shoulder.

"Thank you. Sophie, you are naturally perfect."

Then David stood up and cleared his throat.

"The Perfect Institute is coming to pick you up tomorrow…

"NOOO!!!!"

"Ssshhh. You won't be here for them to collect you. I've got a plan."

"Go on Dad."

"We will take a visit to The Perfect Institute, tell everyone what horrors they are about to experience and they will not want to stay. They will rebel. Tell all the parents about the experience. They will sue the Perfect Institute and it will be no more." David breathed out heavily after his speech. He then smiled a devious smile.

"Get up at 7:30 tomorrow. Things are going to change Sophie, things are going to change."

That night, Sophie put down her book, and switched on her lamp. She squinted because of the bright light she was not used to. She picked up her alarm, which was on the bedside table, and sat up. She leaned her back on the wooden bed stand. She peered in on the alarm. This alarm was from The Perfect Institute. She had the choice to take it home with her for a souvenir. She happily said yes. She then heard a small whirring noise. She lifted the alarm up to her ear, and the whirring got even louder. She then peered into the alarm. A small lens was turning heavily around inside the block. Sophie's eyes widened. A camera. That's exactly what it was. She was shuddering. In slow, steady movements, she got up and dropped the alarm. She then clambered over to her wardrobe, completely forgetting the slow movements of weariness. She got out her biggest boots and fitted them onto her feet. She stomped over to the alarm and stamped on it heavily. A fizz occurred and then slowly faded away. She stamped on it repeatedly. A tear ran down her cheek as she jumped on it non-stop. She then wrenched off her shoes and, annoyingly they didn't come off. She let out a sob and collapsed onto her bed. She thumped both of her hands, onto the bed and tears poured down her cheeks and she used the beds as a drain, as it absorbed her wet tears.

She then calmed down and took in some big, deep breaths. She slithered under her duvet and tried to fall asleep.

Sophie writhed around. Sweat pouring down her face. Her eyes tightly shut. She turned from left to right. Suddenly, she leapt up and started screaming. She looked around hurriedly, still screaming. She shielded herself from her dream. She was still obviously seeing things. She wiped her forehead and started to calm down. She checked her surroundings. She looked at her wrist, which had a shiny watch planted onto it. It was 1am. Sophie sighed. She shrunk down into her duvet and rethought her dream. It was about a big, tall man, whipping her violently, on the back with a rope with string ends. She was forced against a stake and was viciously attacked by this unknown man. All the staff were unknown, and no one knew the reason behind it. She shuddered under her duvet and curled up into small ball to get warm. She shut her eyes.

Chapter 7

The alarm sound should have gone off. However, for obvious reasons it didn't. David came into the room for her, treading in slowly. He walked to her bed and nudged her gently. Sophie writhed around slowly, and then realised what she was about to do. She snapped her eyes open and sat up in bed. David nodded at her and she nodded back. It was time.

She got out of bed and walked over to her wardrobe. It was full of dresses, smart suits and jewellery. She did not want to wear any of those clothes. Therefore, she did something, which was not *at all* perfect. She clambered over to her drawers, took out a pair of scissors, and walked back over to her wardrobe. She peered in and turned her head left. At the back of her wardrobe, neatly hung up, was a dress, she was never intending to wear. She reached out and grabbed it and laid it out onto the floor. She seized the scissors and started to cut along the dangly bottom of the dress. She made it as if they were shorts and slipped it on. She was ready. She shoved the scissors back into the drawer and hurried out of the door. David was at the bottom of the stairs. Everyone was still asleep as they crept past and through the kitchen. They reached the front door. David took out some keys from his pocket and shoved one aggressively into the lock. The force on the key against the door made it bounce straight back and it plunged to the floor. Sophie and David cringed as it rattled against the wooden tiles. They sighed with relief as no one stirred. David picked up the key and calmly placed it into the lock, he twisted his wrist and then the front door opened.

They made their way through the small front garden. They walked towards the gate and opened it slowly. Sophie had never heard such a loud creek in her entire life. They turned right and walked along pavements. Sophie looked down. She was walking on cracks. Bad luck, she thought. She dodged a couple of cracks and smiled, wishing she could do this when she was younger. David then froze and crouched down. He signalled to Sophie that she should duck down as well. Sophie was confused until she glanced towards the road. A white van was approaching along the road. It had clear, red words printed onto it saying: THE PERFECT INSTITUTE. Sophie was startled, if she had left that house a minute later, then she would be trapped in that van, rewinding her horrible childhood. They carried on walking and turned many lefts and many rights. They finally reached a big dome with the same printed words as on the van. Sophie swallowed. Tears started to form in her eyes. Her heart thudded rapidly as memories floated around her head.

David reassuringly patted her on the shoulder, indicating that it will be alright. They had to make a plan.

"We have to find another way in, other than the front door."

"I agree. Right, here's the plan. You go across the left side of the building, and try to find a door. Meanwhile, I will go across the right side and find another way in."

Sophie nodded, her heart beating rapidly. She tucked her hair nicely around her ears. David nodded back and started to move right. Sophie turned left and started to trudge to the edge of the dome. A door, it can't be that hard to find. It turned out that, it was hard to find. Too hard. Sophie then heard a shout, quickly moving her head to the sound of the gruff voice. A worker. Sophie ran towards where they split up. She ran straight into David with a crash. A worker was coming their way.

"Don't panic Sophie. It's going to be fine."

Sophie was crying, clinging on to David like a koala to a tree. David tried to pull her off, but it was too much. The worker strode towards them. David shoved Sophie off and held her by the shoulders.

"Get a grip, Sophie! Someone is coming towards us and you're crying like a baby! Now stand behind me." Sophie nodded.

The worker was two metres away.

"Hey! Hey! Back up!" David shouted.

The worker carried on walking towards them. David stepped forward a punched him round the cheek. The worker barely flinched. He grabbed David and threw him to the floor. Sophie screamed as the worker beat David heavily. A gush of anger suddenly came pouring out of Sophie as she took off her boot. She ran over and whacked her left boot over the man. He stood up and gently shoved Sophie away.

"Oi! That's my daughter!" David screamed and threw a punch which struck the man hard on the chin. He went down in an instant. David got up and grabbed Sophie.

"Come on, let's find a way in."

There was no other possible door to go in other than the main one. They strode over to it and nodded to each other. Then walked in.

There were lines and lines of children all ready to go out. Parents were starting to arrive.

"We have to do this quickly." Many workers were striding over to them now, all in their fancy white suits. David ran into them knocking them over like a bowling ball clattering over the pins. Sophie ran behind him kicking any workers in sight. She managed to climb up some stairs and onto some high ground.

"Everyone! Stop and listen to me!" Sophie shouted.

The whole room went silent. David was protecting Sophie from any workers.

"This is a horrible place! DO NOT eat the pills. They give you a memory pill and an excitement pill. The memory pill deletes all your bad memory and the excitement pill gets you excited to see your parents. DO NOT take them. You need to escape. Now."

A small boy at the back shouted, "They used to wrap me in barbed wire to make me stop picking my nose."

Another girl with blond hair said, "They used to kick me until I could recite all of *War and Peace.*"

There was a hushed silence amongst the parents.

A boy shouted out, "They tied me to a tree trunk to make me stand up straight."

All the children nodded to each other and ran around the room.

In unison they all shouted:

"WE MUST NEVER FORGET."

"Yes!" Sophie said. She smiled as all the kids started to rebel. The parents were looking in at the pure chaos. They were shouting but it wasn't very clear to hear because of all the noise, such as the babies crying and the kids her age shouting.

Workers were getting pushed over by the children. Sophie grinned. David was fighting. Children were rebelling. Not so perfect now is it?

One year later…

The wrecking ball thumped into The Perfect Institute. All the children from the friendly neighbourhood were watching. They were dressed as they liked, some continued to wear perfect clothes and had neat hair, others wore ripped jeans and messy t-shirts. Some had tidy hair, others looked like bird nests. The point was, it was up to the children how they behaved now.

Sophie grinned. The workers were all arrested and the boss of the 'Not So Perfect Institute' was imprisoned for abuse, torture, lying, cruelty, neglect and so on. Not so perfect after all.

Initially the parents were secretly worried about the closure of The Perfect Institute. They'd have to look after their *own* children. Change nappies. Teach them table manners. Listen to violin practice. But over time it turned out that they rather enjoyed spending time with their own children, perfect or not.

Not all the children turned out to be perfect but that doesn't matter. So long as they are happy in the end, everything will always turn out okay.

Back at Orchard House, Philip was loading the dishwasher and Samuel was playing Fur Elise.

"Oh shut up," said Sophie to her brother, "Can't you play something else you moron."

"Mum!" whined Samuel, "Sophie's being mean to me."

"You're the moron Sophie, you can't even read The Iliad," shouted Philip.

"The Willyad more like," said Sophie, "It's rubbish."

Soon there were sounds of thumping, shrieking and sibling squabbles.

Pamela was sitting quietly in the living room wondering what on earth had happened to her perfect children.

David kissed her forehead and said, "They're happy darling, that's all that matters."

He closed the door and went to join in the scrap. Soon he had all three children on the floor in a big wrestle.

Pamela closed her eyes and whispered to herself, "They used to be so quiet…"

The End

Printed in Great Britain
by Amazon

79796996R10031